SHADOW

AARCHI ADVANI SAINI

ISBN 979-888569972-3

Contents

Aarchi Advani Saini.!
    [ ] Author of the book "The Loads Of Poetry"
    [ ] Social media "Aarchi Advani Saini"
    [ ] Aries, believe in destiny.

[ ] Author of the book "The Loads Of Poetry Part One and Two", "The Journey of Love", "The Way to Love", "The Anonymous", "Let's be Confidante", "New Self", "Error", "The Cabalistic Child ", "Confession", "Dark Dead", "Half Dead", "Faith is All", "Anjaan Ajnabi", "Lifeless Life", and

more.

Aarchi was born in India in 25th March 2002, the daughter of Sanjeev Advani Saini and his wife Mamta Saini.

She becomes one of the youngest author of her hometown Shamli. For this Danik Jagran newspaper covers this news, Later, many news channels interviewed her. So renowned for "The loads of poetry). She has sold the book worldwide, the recipient of numerous prestigious awards in her writing journey. She writes daily columns syndicated throughout the world. Aarchi Advani is well known for her writing on many other platforms. She is also a fantasy and literary fiction author specializing in "Life", as well as her upcoming book "Dream".

She publish her 10th book as her Hindi novel called "papa".

She also hosts a channel where she uses her passion for storytelling. And a background in business to help other creatives navigate their writing. So she is compiling an anthology named, "Of Your Choice", And her publishing journey is another level, she is good at her writing skills, but no one knows how to write books, same with her, but with the passage of time, she grows. When she's not writing or tubing she enjoys listening to books,

Making stories on her own. And love to live in her virtual world.

Shadow

I need to write something but its been days that I have even typed a word. My publisher has been sending me emails everyday asking for an update but I haven't replied back to him. Me the great writer 'Aarav' whose first book sold million copies haven't been able to write a word for his next book for days. Life is always unpredictable, is something I always believe. Here I am sitting down at my usual work chair facing garden when I received an email from my editor. Another one, just what I need for my worst day. My editor wants to set up a meeting with me tomorrow morning, I have sent him an email saying a phone call would do and that I am not interested in meeting anyone at the moment.

Next morning my phone started buzzing on the exact same time mentioned in the email. I picked up the call and said 'Hi'. Editor: 'Hey Aarav, how's everything going?' Me: 'Just fine' Editor: 'Aarav, its been months and you haven't written anything till now' Me: Silence Editor: 'People are waiting for your next book and its really nerve wrecking to answer about you to media. Everyone is expecting an update. We can't keep giving them the same answers' Me: Silence Editor: 'Aarav, I think it's time to consider the option I told you before' Me: 'No' Editor: 'There is nothing wrong in using a ghost writer Aarav. At least try to meet him once.' Me: 'I won't allow anyone to write a story under my name. Do you really think its worth the money I get for that when I lose my self-respect?' Editor: 'ok, let's make a deal Aarav. I have already spoke to a very famous ghost writer. He will come to your place in 3 days and will stay with you for a while. It doesn't mean he will write a story or anything. He will live with you and you can discuss some story plots with him if you want or may be he can help you out with stuff you want' Me: 'I won't open my door to anyone, this is the final warning that I will not let anyone into my place. You will soon get a story' and I hanged up the phone.

After the call, my head started pounding. I decided to take a walk and head to my favourite bookshop nearby. I love this bookshop as they collect antique books from 1900's. As I was going around the shop, I saw a book sitting on the table. It felt as if I can see an aura around the book. I took the book in my hand and the title is 'PEN'. I could feel my heart beat while I turned the book around to check the author. Book was written in 1924 and the author name was 'The Trio for freedom'. I couldn't find a name elsewhere. I paid for the book and returned home. I googled the book name and the name listed as author; no results appeared. I placed the book on the table and headed to bed to have a nap as I had a very long day.

I woke up with the sound of doorbell and when I opened the door, I saw a man in his late 20's dressed up in a suit. Being a man myself I couldn't stop wondering how could someone be so handsome. I asked him who he is? He just smiled and came into the house. I told him, 'hey, who do you think you are to barge into my house?'. He just kept smiling and started looking around the house. Then I remembered what editor said about a ghost writer coming to live in the house with me. I turned to him and asked 'are you the ghost writer editor said about. I am sorry you came down but I can't let you stay here. Please leave.' He just smiled and said 'Let me at least introduce myself. I am Bhushan and my friend I don't think I can leave'. His words made me furious and I said, 'what the heck? I said leave.' Bhushan: 'My friend, I know you are not able to write these days. Let me just stay with you and I'll not help you unless you want me to' Me: 'why are you even here now? Editor said that you will be here after 3 days' Bhushan: 'Unfortunately my contract with my old living arrangement has been completed today and I don't have anywhere else to go for the next 3 days' Me: 'Look Bhushan, you look decent enough to understand what I am about to say now.

I don't want any help with my book or doesn't want you to write a book for my fame so please leave' Bhushan with a smile: 'My friend, I completely understand you but let me stay with you till I arrange a new accommodation for me. Right now, I am broke and I don't have a place to go. I promise I won't talk about your story or book at all.'

Somehow, he convinced me, I don't know if its his words or if it's his face or his situation right now, I just agreed for him to stay with me. I showed him the guest room and made it clear that he needs to leave soon and that this is only for temporary.

Once I came back to my bedroom, I started wondering why he doesn't have any luggage and the way he talks is so old fashioned. Who says 'my friend' these days? I told myself, 'this is only temporary, he will leave soon'. Next morning by the time, I woke up I couldn't find him anywhere around. I had my breakfast and sat before my laptop to write. That's when I heard him coming from upstairs with a new suit. I asked him, 'I looked for you and thought you weren't home'. Bhushan: 'I did go out but came back when you were in your room' I thought maybe he went out to grab his luggage as I now see him in a new suit. Me: 'why can't you wear comfortable clothes if you aren't heading anywhere' Bhushan: 'this is the most comfortable clothing for me.' I sighed and turned back to my laptop. I waited for 2 hours but I couldn't write anything. During this time, I kept an eye on what Bhushan's doing. He just went around the living room couple of times and then started checking books in my personal library. He picked up the book I bought yesterday and sat in a chair behind me.

For the next 2 hours he was lost in his thoughts having the book in his lap. I called his name out asking if he is hungry. He said no. I fixed myself a sandwich and told him he can help himself if he is hungry. He just nodded with a smile. I asked him, 'how do you like the book?' pointing to the book on his lap. Bhushan: 'what about you?' Me: 'I haven't even started reading it yet.' Bhushan: 'I know this book by heart. I can tell each and every word from this book'. I couldn't believe him. I took the book from him and opened a page and asked him to say something from page no.250. He started saying the lines from that page. I was surprised by how accurate the lines are. He started laughing aloud after seeing my startled expression. Bhushan: 'its my favourite book, I have read it heaps of time that I now remember each and every part of it' Me:' do you know anything about the author.' Bhushan: 'yes, I do. But I think if you read this book you would know him too. He is a great friend of mine.' Me: 'what? This book is written in 1924.' Bhushan: 'ha ha ha doesn't you feel you know the author sometimes when you read their books. And I feel he is my good friend'. I didn't understand his logic but I felt he might be a huge fan of this book so I didn't want to hurt his feelings.

*

The rest of the day went unusually well with Bhushan's jokes and stories. Most of his stories include his friends and their conversations. I was quite surprised to learn that I had a very good day with him. By the time I was on bed I opened the book 'pen' and started reading....

Based in the time of 1920's, I am walking on the streets with a book and a newspaper. I went into a building and before entering into the building I looked around one more time to make sure no one is following me. I went upstairs and knocked 3 times on a door. The door is opened, I went inside and locked the door behind me. When I turned around, I saw Bhushan there on a table typing something on a typewriter. I went to him and placed today's newspaper in front of him and asked 'is this you?' the newspaper headlines read a British van has been hustled and firearms are stolen killing the British general 'Harry'. He smiled.

I said, 'Bhushan, there is a reason why we call ourselves a trio, you cant go ahead and do something like this without a plan and mess up the things' Bhushan: 'Chandu, would you say yes if I say that we need to do this' Me: 'NO' Bhushan: 'that is the reason why I didn't discuss it with you'. I sat on the chair with a deep sigh and asked 'where is Hassan?'. Bhushan: 'he will be here soon but listen me out, that general Harry has been making things worse for the villagers. So, I didn't have a choice than to kill him as he need to be stopped' Me: 'I understand but everyone is going through hardships due to this British. That is why we need a plan and when we do something, we should at least try to make a difference. What would you do if you get caught by acting rashly without a plan?' Bhushan laughed out loud.

I woke up suddenly and felt that my throat had gone dry. I drank water trying to recall when did I slept reading the book and thought what I had was a dream. Then I saw the book besides me and realised maybe I am re-enacting what I have read in the book. I smiled to myself and went back to sleep. The next morning, by the time I came downstairs to the living room Bhushan was sitting in the sofa in a new suit and lost in deep thoughts. I wished him Good morning and he gave me his usual smile. Even though it's just a day that I have spent with him, I got addicted to his smile. Its like a cool breeze when you need air.

Today I sat before him and started asking questions about him. He didn't say much about what he is doing now and didn't ask me anything either. I thought he must be a private person who would like to keep things for himself. Even today we had a great time. Bhushan really know how to tell stories and make other people laugh. I spent the entire day talking to him. I didn't realise its bed time and came upstairs to sleep. I opened the book again to read…

In the same room, me and Bhushan are having tea discussing about the paper on the wall. We heard three knocks on the door and knew Hassan is there to join us. The moment he stepped in, he just greeted us and sat on the chair nearby. Me and Bhushan sat opposite to him. Hassan: 'Chandu, how's the book going? Do you think it will be ready before our mission?' Me: 'yes, we have 5 more days to our mission and the book will be ready by tomorrow. Bhushan, will your father publish our book?' Bhushan: 'I told my father that I will give him manuscript and made him promise that the books should be published at any cost.' Hassan: 'guys, aren't you going to regret doing this? you guys come from a very rich background where you don't face any issues with British. If we haven't met at the law school and if you haven't accompanied me to all those revolutionary meetings…' Before Hassan could complete Bhushan started talking 'Yes, if we haven't accompanied with you then we wouldn't be part of this great deeds. The moment I saw happy tears in the people when we do something to the Britishers I felt that I was born to do this.' I just smiled looking them. We started discussing our plan for our next mission to kill General Lockwood when he is coming to the village to collect tax.

The day has arrived and we took oath to kill ourselves if in case we were caught. Our plan was to use a bomb on the troops but kill Lockwood by beheading him. No one else knew our plan except us three. And even us we divided the plan to execute it. My part was to deviate the troops by confronting them as a rebel. During this time a bomb would be used by Hassan to create ruckus while Bhushan confront Lockwood and behead him. I did my part of deviating the troops and while I am fighting with the soldiers, a bomb was used and amidst all of this I saw Bhushan facing Lockwood. But as I expected he didn't kill him but was talking to his brother besides Lockwood. I could see Hassan heading towards Lockwood with a pistol but he was shot by Lockwood when Bhushan was standing in front of him. I was already stabbed by the British and was held hostage.

I couldn't believe what I am seeing, Bhushan is still talking to Lockwood and his brother. I clearly understood that me and Hassan was betrayed. I bit the cyanide held to my neck and the last thing I saw before I closed my eyes were Bhushan looking at me.

I woke up again with sweat and felt that my throat is dry again. I couldn't imagine having a similar dream as the previous day and even now I couldn't recall when I slept reading the book. It took me sometime to go back to sleep again. The next day when I headed down, I saw Bhushan standing facing to the garden. I wished him good morning and told him about the dreams I had from the last 2 nights. He just smiled. I asked him if that is the end of the story. Bhushan: 'No, the story ends with Bhushan dying'. I turned around and asked him 'why did he die? He is the one who betrayed his friends.' Bhushan:' should I tell you the remaining story then?' I am too excited to know what happened later on but I told him that I'll read it myself. He smiled and as usual we had a great day. I never thought that hanging with some unknown could be this fun. By night when I was heading to my room Bhushan said 'My friend, remember that I always love you. Good night'. Me: 'can't you please stop using all those old phrases as if you are in your 90's and please stop wearing those goddamn suits. I am now having nightmares of you in your suits' Bhushan just laughed out loud.

I got settled down on bed and took the book in hands...

Bhushan was talking to his brother. 'brother, why are you here?' His brother: 'I came to talk business with Mr. Lockwood. why are you doing this? I'll talk to Lockwood and this will be like it never happened with no punishment to you' Bhushan: 'You need to turn around brother before you see how cruel your brother can be' While he is talking, Lockwood shot Hassan. Bhushan: 'Did you see brother, what he has done to my friend. I want you to move aside before I kill you too.' That's when Bhushan turned his head to see Chandu killing himself. That was the last straw he could take. He took his sword out and beheaded Lockwood with one blow. His brother panicked and started running away. Before he was held captive by the British soldiers, he shot himself.

We were infamously called "the trio' who killed the general that ordered to rape all the women in the village including children. The book 'pen' was published by Bhushan's father but was blacklisted as its serving as a motivation to people to join the revolution.

I woke up with the thudding sound and realised its already 9AM in the morning. The doorbell is ringing so I came downstairs to open the door. A man in his 40's greeted me. I asked him, 'who are you?' Man: 'I am the ghost writer sir. My name is Sam. Editor asked me to meet you here today' Me: 'what do you mean? The writer is already here 3 days ago.' He seems to be quite confused and took his phone out. I started looking around for Bhushan while he was on phone but couldn't see him anywhere. The new guy passed me his phone for me to talk to Editor. Editor: 'Aarav, I know you don't want a ghost writer but just let him in' Me:' what are you talking about? Bhushan was already here 3 days ago' Editor: 'Aarav, I haven't sent anyone named Bhushan'. I hung up the phone and ran upstairs. There is no one in the bedroom and the bed was well made. I realised I didn't take any details from Bhushan. I sat on the bed with my head between my hands.

That night when I went to bed, I am still confused why Bhushan left with out saying goodbye. I took the book to finish it today as one of the reasons being its Bhushan's favourite book...

Bhushan is talking to me, 'my friend, my brother, I would never betray you... I couldn't forget the look in your eyes during your last breath... I have always been around you and waited for one chance to explain myself of what happened that day. And I think I have told you what you need to know now. This book 'pen' was written by you. I think God helped me by giving one last chance to talk and spend time with you.

Brother if at all I am reincarnated I wish to be born as your brother again and be part of 'the trio'. Love you my friend...'

I woke up with tears on my cheeks. I couldn't believe what I just heard. I took the book in my hands and saw the author name 'The Trio for the freedom'. I opened the book and the book consist of interviews by revolutionary groups. It doesn't have any of the story I dreamt or read about. I now know what I saw in the dreams are what Bhushan want me to know. I closed my eyes and recalled all the beautiful moments with him.

1 year later:

I was in my garden when I my phone started buzzing. I answered the call

Publisher:' Aarav, you did it again. We sold 10 million copies of your book: 'The Trio''. I smiled.

A cool breeze touched my face and I could feel that
Bhushan is smiling too...

Bonus Poem

A fun convo.

Will you be here?

Where?

Here?

Where?

Here.

Why so doubtful?

Nothing's real. On the verge of fading.. fading.. fading.. and gone.

Even about yourself?

Unreal for someone out there. Fingers crossed that it isn't me.

I belong here anyway?!

Now.. today? And there is tomorrow we don't know about.

Keep my place reserved, will you?

Never had any. It's all full with um no one but many. I'm sorry?

No, you aren't. I'd still be here. Somewhere in the corner. Smiling. Waiting.

For?

You.

Where will I be?

Will you be here?

Here?

Here.

I don't forget things. Prolly make sure things don't let me forget them. Seeps in. Leaks in. Crawls in.

And what if you forgive the way?

I was never mad at it. I'm just always..

The h in a hug stands for hurt; the h in a heart stands for hollowness.

Um. The h in hurt stands for habit; the h in hollowness stands for heaviness.

The h in home stands for hatred.

Stop.

Why?

You're being h for hopeless.

And you always play along.

One mississippi, two mississippi, three mississippi.. Where are youuu?

Breathes

Breathes along

No one's gonna find you if not me.

I know.

Your weird and tired.

I know.

You're afraid of looking into yourself now.

I know.

You need help.

I know.

You're not you.

I know.

You.. I.. Fck it.

Hahah. Caught you. Caught you but.. unable to hold you.

That's alright. Flowers hurt more than thorns. Sky hurts more than ground. Lalalalala.

What?

Grey. Her eyes are grey?

Tf?

I never knew? He must have known right? Was I even supposed to look into them? They.. they were hurt, hollow and heavy. They are light grey? I never knew!

Idk what's this but flowers heal and sky is hope.

Oh, is it so? I'll never know.

And I'm hopeless?

You'll never know either.

Breathes

Sobs

Flowers. The last thing she could offer. Sky. The last place she'd ever want to look for him.

Chuckles

Stop.

Chuckles

I said stop?!

I hate you.

Fine. Atleast you stopped.

Temporarily.

I know right. It's all about temporary gains and permanent losses.

l couldn't look into them again.. I wonder if they got their old colour back. Not grey.. colourless.

Are you talking about just the eyes?

Sighs

There are thorns in life and flowers in after. In a blink of an eye, the feet raise above the ground and in second, they'd be flying in the sky. Fun. It's all funny.

But you aren't. Why so serious?

Always been.

You were so when you decided not to cry. "It's enough. No more tears to waste."

Hehe. The universe listened I swear. The very next day, I wasn't even left with any to spend.

What if..

Don't.

What if that differently sleepless night was telling you something?

Telling? Hah! It showed me how morning can be darker.

Darkest.

Yet.

I.. I'm not ready for more such happenings.

No one is.

Does hollowness work?!

Love is done. The damage is done.

Cruel.

What isn't?

Shaving my head.

Don't. They're loved..

It's the only visible weight, darl. What else?

Cruel.

It's raining.

Outside and inside, both?

I hate July.

I get it. Too cold eh?

Coldest. And the worst part? Our warmest clothes, froze. I can remember the smiles when we wore them. These are the type of smiles which make you cry worse.

Go away.

From?

Me.

You won't be fine.

I never was.

For?

Some time?

Sure. Can't promise but I'll take care.

Lies. Lies.

Um thing is..

I know. I know you've left quite ago. I know you aren't here anymore but I wish you be back to me.

I'm sorry. For everything.

Travel to the places that won't welcome you and leave a smile there. Be back someday?

Someday.

Where?

Here?

Here.

I love everything

Fire's spreading all around my room

My world's so bright

It's hard to breathe but that's alright

Hush.